Dinosaur Dug
The World's Smartest Dude

ASPERGER'S SYNDROME (AUTISM)

Written by Jill Bobula and Katherine Bobula • Illustrated by Rob Hall

Wildberry
Productions

www.wildberryproductions.ca

Brought to you by Wildberry Productions
as part of the WE ARE POWERFUL® children's series.

WE ARE POWERFUL®

ISBN 978-0-9784095-6-2

Text copyright © 2008 by Wildberry Productions.
Illustration copyright © 2008 by Wildberry Productions.
WE ARE POWERFUL ® 2008 by Wildberry Productions.
Desktop publishing by Janine Frenken.
Photography by George Karam.
Edited by Nicole Dion.

www.wildberryproductions.ca

Wildberry Productions would like to recognize the Lowe-Martin Group for their generous support of the WE ARE POWERFUL® children's series and their contribution toward children's mental and neurological health issues.

Printed by The Lowe-Martin Group
Printed in Canada

First Wildberry Productions printing, October 2008.

This book is dedicated to everyone touched by Asperger's syndrome.

"Here is one of my most vivid memories of school; I am standing in a corner of the playground as usual, as far away as possible from people who might bump into me or should, gazing into the sky and absorbed in my own thoughts. I'm eight or nine years old and have begun to realize that I am different in some nameless but all-pervasive way."

– Claire Sainsbury, *Martian in the Playground*, Lucky Duck Books,
© Claire Sainsbury, 2000, Reprinted with Permission of SAGE

"Not everything that steps out of line, and thus 'abnormal', must necessarily be 'inferior'."

– Hans Asperger

My name is Diego and I'm the world's smartest dude. I know a lot about dinosaurs. Some people call me Dinosaur Diego. I have Asperger's syndrome, a form of autism. I love who I am because I'm such a great kid! My Asperger is a very precious gift.

Asperger means my brain works a little differently than my family and friends. Keep reading and find out what makes me so special.

At school, I'm called the whiz kid. That's because I'm very smart. In fact, I'm the smartest person in my school. Not all people who have Asperger are as smart as me.

I love dinosaurs and reading about them excites me. I could read and read and read about them. Ask me anything about dinosaurs and I just might know the answer.

Did you know that a Diplodocus is a dinosaur that lived to 100 years old? And did you know it lived on our planet 150 million years ago? A Diplodocus has a neck and a tail longer than my house!

The dinosaur's nostrils were at the top of its head. Hhmmm...I'm not sure what happens when it rains though. Does the rain fall into his nostrils? Do his nostrils close when it rains? If they do, how does he breathe? I haven't found the answer yet, but I'm still searching.

Because I have Asperger, I often focus on my favorite subject, dinosaurs. My friends aren't as excited about dinosaurs as I am and sometimes they walk away from me because that's all I talk about.

I like spending time with some friends, but I also like being alone. Sometimes when I'm with other people, I feel a little strange and different. Mom and dad tell me this is part of my Asperger's syndrome.

Friendship is not something I understand very well.
Making friends is not always easy for me. I have to try hard
to feel comfortable around other people.

I know my friends find talking with me hard at times.
Sometimes I don't understand what my friends mean when they talk.

Hannah, one of the girls in my class, likes to tell jokes. My friends laugh at her jokes, but because I have Asperger, I don't always get it.

When people say things, I believe every word they say. The other day, Willie said it was raining cats and dogs. Everyone laughed except me. When I looked outside, all I saw was the pouring rain.

I thought about what Willie said for the rest of the afternoon. I couldn't understand what he meant because I have Asperger.

The bus came and all I could think of were cats and dogs and the rain. How can they come down from the sky?

How do cats and dogs get in the sky anyway? Won't they hurt themselves as they fall to the ground?

When I got home, I told my mom Willie said it was raining cats and dogs. She smiled and explained that Willie meant it was raining very hard.

Another part of Asperger's syndrome is that I use different words to express myself than other kids my age. It's not easy for my friends to understand me.

I have a hard time looking at my friends' face when they talk.
I feel nervous and glance at them quickly instead.

I also have a hard time understanding people's facial expressions. My friend Thomas makes faces all the time. He can make 13 different faces. I'm not sure what they mean or why he does that.

My teacher Miss Sage is great. She met with my mom to learn about Asperger's syndrome.

My mom explained to Miss Sage that my brain works differently than the brains of other children. Things like emotions and feelings can be difficult for me to understand.

Hannah tore her favorite blouse on the swing at recess.
I didn't understand why she was so upset because she has other
blouses at home.

Once when our class went to the library, Annie was reading a book on farm animals. My classmates were laughing at a picture of a pig covered in mud and dirt. I didn't think it was funny.

Lights, sounds and smells affect me because of Asperger's syndrome.

My mom removes all the tags from my clothing because they bother me. Some of my friends wished their parents would take out the tags from their clothes because it also irritates them. But they don't have Asperger.

I feel nervous when there's a lot of activity or a lot of people around me. When I'm nervous, I like to rock myself. It's hard for my parents and my teacher to see me like that because they know it's not easy for me to leave my safe world.

My classmates are great. They understand Asperger's syndrome and they're always there to help me. When the noise in class gets loud, Hannah will tell the teacher. Miss Sage will then ask my classmates to be more quiet.

Although having Asperger's syndrome is not easy, my friends and family are there to help me. One day while I was waiting for the bus, an older boy came up to me and started teasing me because I have Asperger's syndrome.

Eddy stood by my side and told the boy to stop bullying me. My mom said she was glad Eddy was my friend.

I know having Asperger's syndrome makes me different. Although I'm the smartest student in my school, I have to get better at how I talk and behave with others. I may know a lot about dinosaurs, but I'm still learning about people.

There are moments when I live in my own world, but I still live with all of you most of the time. I'm proud of who I am. I don't mind people knowing I have Asperger's syndrome. After all, my intelligence is a gift. Some of the nicest people of all time have Asperger. I think I'm a very special person.

The "WE ARE POWERFUL®" children's book series was conceived and designed to introduce the lives of eight children affected with various disorders, syndromes and learning disabilities. Each book brings to light the experiences of these children affected with Attention Deficit Hyperactivity Disorder, Attention Deficit Disorder, Tourette Syndrome, Obsessive Compulsive Disorder, Asperger's Syndrome, Fetal Alcohol Spectrum Disorder, Dyslexia and Dyspraxia.

The books familiarize the reader with the daily joys and challenges these children experience in their home and school setting. Children affected by these disorders, syndromes and learning disabilities are gifted in many ways. The "WE ARE POWERFUL®" children's book series was written to help children, parents, educators, health practitioners and the public in general develop a greater understanding of each condition.

Katherine Bobula is a registered nurse with a Bachelor in the Science of Nursing and a Masters in Education. She is an international speaker and consultant specializing in children's mental and neurological conditions including learning disabilities. Katherine has a special interest in Asperger's Syndrome and Fetal Alcohol Spectrum Disorder. She is also a certified presenter for the Tourette Syndrome Foundation of Canada.

Jill Bobula is a graduate of psychology from McGill University. She is a speaker for the Tourette Syndrome Foundation of Canada and is an advocate for children's mental and neurological health issues. Jill's son has Tourette Syndrome Plus.

Katherine, Jill and Rob